Dream Dogs

By ~~Kristy Web~~ster

6-27-2015

Dear Susan + Cindy,

I'm so happy to have you both in my life.

With Love,

Kris

Acknowledgements

I Once Knew, Sirens

Dream Dog, Molotov Cocktail

The Conscience of Spiders, GirlChildPress

SheWolf, GirlChildPress

The Message, Ginger Piglet

Graduation, ThickJam

Brothers, Abacot Journal

Guppy Suicides, Connotation Press

The Hunchback Shops at Safeway, Connotation Press

The Sisters, Connotation Press

Birth, Molotov Cocktail

The Need, Pacifica Literary Review

The Goods, Pithead Chapel

Dedicated to and in memory of Lauren Simonutti; artist, photographer and inspiration.

"I used to think I was the strangest person in the world but then I thought there are so many people in the world, there must be someone just like me who feels bizarre and flawed in the same ways I do. I would imagine her, and imagine that she must be out there thinking of me too. Well, I hope that if you are out there and read this and know that, yes, it's true I'm here, and I'm just as strange as you."

–Frida Kahlo.

Table of Contents

I Once Knew

1.

The Shadow

I once knew a woman with no arms who fell in love with a man who had no legs. The shadow of their naked embrace resembled a spider. He boiled her noodles cooked al dente, how she preferred them. She carried him on her back so he could see the sunset from their porch. When he died, her body started to absorb her legs until they shrunk up inside of her. Her head absorbed what was left of the body until it too, disappeared. When the memory of her love came for her head, it melted her eyes like frozen stars, drowned every last speck of silver from her hair. All but the shadow of the two of them made whole remained.

2.

The Dream

I once knew a Dream who had no idea she was a Dream. She lifted the top of our heads and dipped her toes inside our slick brains. She gently carved into our heads an alphabet of images, some grainy, some sharp and muscular. Each morning our waking destroyed her, but in our sleep she rose again, forgetting what her fevers and floats had left behind, clueless of her repetition. Until one night inside one of our minds she stayed trapped, the images collapsing upon her. Night after night, she apologizes for the death of all other dreams to that tortured dreamer.

3.

The Artist

I once knew a girl afraid of her own breasts. To overcome her fear, she began painting with them. She'd paint the nipple one color, and the rest of her breast indefinable patterns of her own making. Her paintings quickly became the talk of the art class. Though her bare breasts still frightened her, she loved how when she pressed her paint stained bosom to the canvas, paper, or wood, they resembled wildflowers, and sunflowers, a bright and thirsty garden.

The Leaving

The danger in being touched by such a gentle and confident ghost was that she'd fear death even less. But because she was more alone than she could possibly bear, she called to him by name and he responded by lifting her up inside the dark air of her room. She closed her eyes, and let her entire body relax as she levitated off the floor. The ghost spun her in the air like a seasoned dance partner. Before long, the other world called to him to return. Softly, in his arms she descended and touched the cold floor again. When he disappeared, she was left with a fresh sort of sadness that after a few days felt like love.

The Mother Song

The man returned to his wife after seven months. He'd left to find himself and locate the love he'd lost for her, but by then, it was too late.

The wife had taken her two boys, one on her back, one by the hand, and returned to her father's country. There she ate potatoes and shellfish by the sea. Her aunts and uncles fed her legacies and legends, infused her and made her whole again with tales of her ancestors.

When the man returned to their empty home, he covered the walls in letters of apology, words that told of his regrets and promised her a life of comfort, the dream of a model husband who'd learned his lesson.

But the wife had shorn the hair from her head and forgotten her husband's touch. The wife bled every month and made herself tea. Wife became Woman, and gathered her children onto her lap and sung them the songs of her father, told them how once her people spoke the language of both beasts and angels alike.

The husband sought out his wife to make a home of her like before. But upon finding her, she offered him the only gift she had left for him: a jar filled with the sand where she'd slept alongside her sons during his absence.

When the man opened the jar, pain escaped. He found himself in those grains, those miniscule but terrifying little worlds.

Dream Dog

These kisses happen in my dreams with men I haven't met, who maybe don't exist at all. Though from everything I've read, our dreams can't create fictitious people. Last night while kissing one of these men our bodies joined at the lips but the rest of our bodies disassembled—a leg floated out the window, a buttocks and a torso rolled into the backseat. Our mouths sucked so hard eventually that was all that was left, just our lips and teeth and tongues as the rest of us disappeared. We did not miss our other parts.

*

I have been looking for a dog. Before the kissing dreams, I had dog dreams. Like the men, the dog may or may not exist. But I dreamed so many dreams about that same dog I am convinced the dog not only exists, but the dog is calling me. I've scoured Craigslist.org logging several hours at work a day. I am looking for a dog on the edge of human, a dog who wants to speak, a dog who knows I am the only one.

*

Cats moan outside my window while the computer screen echoes off my face, my tired eyes. Dogs consume me. Not only my dog, my dream dog, but after hundreds of hours of searching, I feel all dogs are calling me. I can't, I whisper, I can't take you all.

*

This time I cry before the man kisses me because he is so tender. We are enveloped by a warm sphere of light, the bed unfamiliar and soft. He tells me I write what I'm too afraid to speak out loud. A dog barks. A new light wakes me. My face has yet to dry.

*

Four dogs stare up at me, heads tilted, wondering how I manage--so bald, so raw and open. I want so much. All they want is to be fed.

*

All four dogs are ones I was once convinced were my dream dog. But once I brought them home, once I let them on my bed or fed them scraps from my take-out boxes, I came to realize, they were not it. I have found my dogs in overcrowded shelters, Craigslist ads--MOVING CAN'T TAKE SCRAPPY WITH—even tied to fence posts with signs reading "FREE", but nothing is free, not even love. Most of all love. Let alone dreams.

*

It happens the first night of my period. A howl. The dirt smells richer when I bleed. The nights are restless, sometimes the tears are unstoppable and not even the embarrassments of late night talk shows drown them out. The howl is more primal than that of a dog. The howl grows stronger and closer and I know. I understand. But curled up in sheets, soaked with red, my fear is hot and scorching. I don't answer the door. I can't answer the call.

*

A neighborhood child I've always found bothersome is wailing. I cover my gory scene in a fat robe and wander out, half dazed. The mother grabs her child, forces his wet face against her breasts. A dog is dead. Demolished by a careless driver. The dog lays bloody in the middle of the road. My dream dog murdered because of my fear. I am a careless dreamer.

*

This kiss is just as potent but less tender. The teeth are ruthless, the tongue is dangerous and weird. Black. Cold. I wake up mid climax, my four dogs, whining by the bed. They only want to be fed.

The Conscience of Spiders

(In memory of outsider artist Henry Darger.
April 12, 1892 to April 13, 1973)

Before I was a woman, I was a spider. My footsteps
were silent. Cold, dark places were my home. I took what I
needed and left the excess. No one told me what I was. I
was born knowing it all, my purpose, my strength, and my
prey.

Eventually I tired of the basement's dank, moldy
laundry. I wanted to nest in a higher place, to know the
world at a distance, guarding my solitude with anonymity.
That is how I came upon the old janitor.

He was called Henry Darger. I spun a web inside his
apartment window. Other curious spiders joined me and
Henry's quiet audience grew. His apartment never knew
day from night, and no one knew him but us.

We watched him glue portraits of baby-faced girls to
watercolor landscapes stretched across the walls, the floor.
Henry painted his heroes the Vivian Girls--little girls with
penises who fought off monsters and men in military coats.
We his spider daughters argued amongst ourselves. Is he a
deviant or an innocent? Some decided he was the
pornographer gone mad in his isolation. Others like me
decided he was a child, clueless of the rules. The only
undecided Daughter of Darger silently crawled across a
wet painting until she reached the face of an unfinished
pig-tailed girl, and blossomed from the child's mouth like
a tiger lily.

Henry's thick, coarse, and charcoal stained hands are
unspoken evidence of invented magic, places lit by his

imagination. That's when I envied the dreaming. Henry, in your dreams do the little girls defeat the evil monsters in the Glandolinian War? In your dreams have you spotted me, your protector of secrets?

Henry's life took place on pages, tens of thousands of pages. But sometimes words were spoken into the deceivingly empty apartment. One year Henry cursed God for the snow, cursed the church for leaving him both fatherless and childless. These are moments I was tempted to reveal myself, but I knew Henry was a maker, something more than an ordinary man, capable of creating his desired company. I was superfluous.

In Henry's room, there were no empty bottles of liquor or wine, no excess articles of clothing strewn about the room. And in the thousands of pictures piled, stacked and sometimes scattered, there were no traces of Henry's past, only the traced, drawn and painted faces of his little girl heroines, the pillars of his blooming story.

Henry is a snowflake in hell. My capsule of a body carries the hot poison that could melt him. But I want him to finish and I want the little girls to steal the waves of grass back from the dragons and soldiers. I want to know that the littlest beings can show the Giants the secret places they've been missing.

Thousands of water colored pages later, our Henry dies in his sleep. Not on his mattress which was buried in pages, but in his chair, at his desk, still in navy-blue janitor overalls, his hands and head resting on his latest collage of the Vivian Girls, who'd claimed the final victory.

People enter his sanctuary, our sanctuary. Strangers interpret the old janitor's room. A woman in a pompous yellow hat calls him a recluse. The word rings true, resonates with me. I am the same. I spring towards the yellow to become a star atop the woman's hat. I am invisible, her worst fear.

Little did I know that once I released my venom into the woman's skin, I'd be caught and killed and this would be my last life as a spider, a small, unnoticed predator. If I had known that I would be reborn as the very same thing I poisoned, would I have let the strangers interpret our Henry's works without interference?

In my new body I am a clumsy mess. Now gaudily visible I can no longer disappear into cracks, or make homes of windowsills and curtains. Even houses won't conceal me.

Though I'm a woman now, I sometimes remember having been very small, and having hung from high places. In my home the smallest, most hidden places take precedence and I welcome silent visitors. The venom of my new existence is Time. I wait for the next rebirth. I ache for a transformation to be once again a selective danger.

A Letter to My Friend Who is Dying

I know a lot more than you think I do, for instance, I know that you are going to die very soon. I've known since early March, the day you had your ladies over for poker, remember? I do because that night I ate salmon and you know how salmon is my favorite. I smelled something each time I walked close to you, every time you touched me. I struck you out of fear, because you didn't smell like you. You had the scent of a wandering stranger, far from home, far from health. The thin skin on your wrist where I scratched you tore a little. You bled, and when you bled, I knew without a doubt. Your blood has been screaming with it ever since.

When you die, I'll be sent to live with your sister Mona, or as I call her MOAN-a. I'll have to put up with her horrible little dogs; the ones that she lets lick her face for an awkward length of time. Under her guardianship, I'll end up hiding in the spare room all day, missing the garden. In the garden I feel like the world belongs to just us. You sit in your cedar bench, with your yellow sunhat and your books. I still sit by your side every afternoon, even now that you smell like a dead mole, like dog's breath, like the kitchen when the food is left out overnight. You're tired, more than usual, but you haven't caught on yet. No one has but me.

That time I spent a week at Mona's home--I still haven't forgiven you for that just so you know-- she was watching one of her favorite programs. It was hosted by a man who could read minds and tell people things they didn't know. He'd pick random audience members and tell them their dead dad or aunt or mother or father said to move on, where they left the secret stash of money, or how they really died. Mona sat on the couch with her ghastly little dogs, her pug, her yorky, and worst, her bug eyed Chihuahua donning a pink tutu and matching collar. Mona cried when the people on TV cried and she took down the number at the end of the show because I guess she wants that strange man to tell her things she doesn't know.

Why would anyone want to know about something they can do nothing about? I know that you will die, and I know that your death will be painful. I can smell the pain. I didn't need a strange man with orange skin to tell me. When you know someone, the way I know you, the truth of things will find a forgotten place inside you to crawl inside of and to whisper, "This is how it will be, this is what will happen." Mona wants to know something she doesn't. I would un-know what I know if I could.

When you die, no one else in the world will see what you see in me, what you've always seen. How long have I lived with you, seventeen years? Since I was a tiny little thing. Remember how terrified I was? I hid under the covers. I hid in corners and dark cabinets. When you are gone, I will be that terrified again, maybe even more. So I've decided what will happen to me when you die: I will join you.

I'm not sure how to do it yet. I don't want to die a gruesome death, but I don't want to die like a coward either. Don't think I'm romanticizing the taking of my own life, or your untimely death. I'm being pragmatic. You see, I've had a lovely time with you, quite lovely, lovelier than I ever imagined. Why live out the rest of my years without you, you who made my world so lovely?

I know you've been worried for me, thinking I'm the one with only a little time left, afraid that I will leave you. Don't worry my friend. I'll be here right until the end. Nurses and fair-weather friends, Mona and her bulimic dogs, they will come and go. Not me. I will be here until the last breath and then I will follow you into the ominous Next Place.

When you die there will be no one left for me, not really. Someone—maybe Mona, maybe not-- may feed me, give me shelter, and occasionally attempt to show me affection in spite of my hostility. But no one will ever look at me again and think, "There's my friend, my very best friend." Once you're gone they will say, "There goes that old black cat, that stuck up cat with the long, gray whiskers," they will say, "How old is he anyway? Probably doesn't have much time left." I know I have more time than they would ever guess. At least, I would if I had you to grow old with. But I won't because the disease is taking over you, and it will continue eating you up until there's more disease than you.

For as aloof and independent as you believe me to be, I am quite fond of you. That is why I will follow you, purring, weaving between your legs, and I will never leave your side. Everyone should have that someone who never, ever leaves their side, no matter what. I will go with you, because you are the lady who calls me Friend, when the rest of the world calls me Cat.

Sticks and Stones

Today I comforted a wounded stranger in a purple hat with a Webster's Dictionary. Her pride had been ripped apart by an adjective, her crime committed in just two words: handsome lamp.

"My friend said I can't use handsome to describe anything but a man."

"Phooey on your friend," I told her.

"Yes, phooey," she said, "but it really bummed me out."

That's when the old woman in the purple hat started to cry, right there in the bookstore, while holding the Webster's Dictionary in her trembling hands.

"You can use handsome however you want," I told her. When she sat, I patted her back.

I agree that a lamp can be handsome. I believe a man can be beautiful. I know sometimes monsters are precious while most angels are terrifying.

Shewolf

Evie's mother refused to teach her how to use a sewing machine. She told her, "Evie, you might let the thread tangle. You might undo good work and replace it with not so good work. You might press the foot pedal too hard. Even worse, you might catch your fingers in the machine. That would be awful, wouldn't it? To sew over your hand?" The "mights" grew mightier and mightier.

This meant Evie had to sew by hand. She started with doll clothes, and little pillows made from scraps of outgrown slips. Any risks would float up to the ceiling like iridescent bubbles.

Evie's father refused to teach her how to mow the lawn. "You might run the mower over your mother's flower bed. You could destroy her lilacs, her daffodils, her tulips. Your mother would be so upset. You might hit a rock and the rock could ricochet into your eye. Worse yet, you might run the mower over your own foot. Think, all the bad things that could happen. How awful!"

Evie watched her brother mow the lawn on Tuesday afternoons when he didn't have soccer practice. She was still sewing but now she sewed dolls in bed. The dolls were made from old socks and they all looked like Evie. Evie had not done this on purpose.

*

Evie learned to draw and she didn't draw horses. She drew sad, naked women. She drew men without faces. She started with graphite, and later she learned about charcoal. The great thing about charcoal is that it blends and smears. Say you wanted to watch one those sad, naked women through a window, and stare into her tragic gray eyes. You could smear the charcoal lines of the windowsill and use your finger to plant diagonal streaks across the glass. That way the woman could remain a mystery. This means someone might be intrigued and ask you about it.

Evie's high school art teacher asked Evie if she wanted to learn how to paint. That's when the "mights" came back. Because, imagine, what happens when you think you can paint but you really can't. Think about what might happen if you splattered paint, accidentally, on someone else's shoes. At first she might say, "No biggie." But you'd know in the weeks to come that it really was a biggie because she'd pretend to not see you in the cafeteria and when she did make eye contact, she'd immediately whisper something to the student standing near them.

No. Charcoal is good. What you don't want them to see you can just smear.

*

The curly-haired guy she slept with kept asking, "Do you want to be my girl?"

Evie lied and said Yes. But the window was open and she snuck out before sunrise.

Before she left, she wrote him a note and stuck it on his dresser. The drawers of the dresser were plastered with stickers. You'd think he'd be shy about all those gold fire department stickers and the one of the Mystery Mobile. Maybe this had been his dresser since he was in third grade. Maybe this piece of childhood furniture reminded him of something really great, something he couldn't bear to forget. She doubted it though. People don't keep things that long. Goodwill, that's it. It's probably from Goodwill.

The note she left the guy had a phone number on it, but it wasn't Evie's. That is, by one number it wasn't. The last digit of her phone number is six, not nine. He might try that though. He might get it right just by guessing, and then he might ask, "Well are you my girl?" His dog barked as she climbed out the window. The dog, a black and white Australian Shepherd with a stolen face.

*

"Guess what?" Evie asked the Mystery Mobile boy.

"What?"

"I'm leaving you for someone who understands me."

So Evie left and when she did she took her dream journal with her.

This other man could decipher dreams and most times he'd tell her that all her dreams were about sex. At first she believed him, but more and more it depressed her. She once had a dream that she was in charge of caring for a great number of phoenixes and Evie thought this was one dream that he couldn't say was about sex. Not possibly.

"Well," he told her, "really, there is only one Phoenix, not a whole bunch."

"So?"

"But it's still an important dream. It means you rise above bad things." He told her.

He could have said she "transcended great difficulties." Did he actually believe Evie wasn't smart enough to get a word like "transcend"? He might have mentioned it to some of his college friends later, like, to mock her, to make fun of her. It might not be so bad to be with someone who doesn't understand you. But this guy, he left no windows open because he was always so cold. Evie thought this was because he was too thin and had nothing to insulate his flat body.

The only thing left to do was to claw, bark and bite, until, finally, he begs her to leave. And finally, he did.

*

The great thing lying is that people believe you. Evie especially enjoyed lying about her name. She'd always had an attachment to the name Maria. She loved how when she introduced herself to strangers, she could see the relief on their faces when they heard something familiar. Maria like the mother of God, or Maria from Westside Story. Sometimes she'd go overboard and say her name was Persephone or Antigone. Still, people believed that, and she liked it.

The bad thing about being a liar is trying to remember what lies you've told and whom you told the lies to. That's not so easy. For example if person A meets person B and they are both talking about Evie but one of them calls her Maria, and the other calls her Antigone, they might get a clue and think Evie wasn't really such hot stuff after all. That might mean Evie would have to stop lying, and that'd be too bad, because she really, really enjoyed herself.

Sometimes though, when you're kissing some hot man on the sidewalk and it's pouring down rain like in that ending scene in Breakfast at Tiffany's, sometimes it's not so romantic and it's better to tell the truth. It's better to say, "I don't like this. I'm cold."

*

The great thing about being gone is you never have to explain why you left. Sure, someone might look for you and actually find you, but then you could act like it's been so long, you don't recognize his face. Wouldn't they feel embarrassed? Probably, he would forget you and buy his milk and cigarettes and that'd be the end of it.

The bad thing about leaving is you might not ever hear about how some people miss you. That is, if you do the kind of leaving that you are still alive afterwards. Some people don't do it like that, so what does it matter? But if you're still around somewhere other than where those people live, you might wish you knew if they were talking about you and wondering where you went. It might be, no one cares and wouldn't that be awful? If you thought it was so important to leave, and then, come to find out, nobody cared anyway? Then you might want to do the other kind of leaving.

Evie likes fishing, almost as much as she likes lying. Her father never taught her to fish, on account of she might put a fishhook through her hand, or fall into the water, she might drown and trout would nibble off chunks of her skin. Someone would eventually find her, some old fisherman maybe, and wouldn't that be awful? A poor old fisherman finding a half eaten girl at the bottom of the river?

This isn't the case though. When Evie goes fishing, she might catch a fish, she might not. She might fall into the water and if she did, she'd swim back to her boat. She might watch the ripples in the water and see Persephone, Antigone, Maria or, she might see the woman in the window, behind the smeared charcoal.

The Late Bloomer

Maggie played keyboard and sang at local farmers markets on Saturdays and sometimes at coffee shops. She stood out for a girl her age because she didn't wear tight jeans and glittery t-shirts. She kept her raven colored hair in chin length ringlets. She wore dresses that were fitted and lovely, modest and nostalgic, dresses that reminded older people of softer times. She carried an air much bigger, broader than her generation did collectively. She appeared sweet, but thick with purpose.

The first time Abby noticed Maggie, Maggie was singing and playing during the 4th of July. Abby handed her a twenty dollar bill for her homemade C.D. and when Maggie reached for her coin purse, Abby insisted "No, keep the change. Try some of that strawberry-rhubarb pie in the next booth." After her next set Maggie did just that. She never thought of Abby while eating the pie. She thought of strawberries and sun and butter. She contemplated the strange carved out clouds that hovered over the town, threatening to cut short the outdoor celebration. But she did not think of Abby.

Abby listened to Maggie's CD's twenty times the first day. She thought of Maggie every day. Thoughts of Maggie lead to thoughts of youth and sex but mostly youth. Nostalgia set in among those thoughts and bit the insides of her belly. She had very little rummaging to do to find the picture she ached for. It was pressed between the pages of her copy of The Little Prince. A picture of a petite little boy dressed in overalls two sizes too small, a bearded man with his hand on the little boy's shoulder, a Gothic looking and skinny woman with her hands clasped together at her waist. The photo elicited no sighs of joy, but it worked. The gnawing in her belly had stopped.

***

A few months after their meeting during 4th of July Maggie left Glory Town to attend her first year of college where she majored in Music and English. Maggie was the sweetheart of her family. Though she had two siblings, and older brother and older sister whom could have easily succumbed to jealousy and envy they too adored Maggie. Maggie and her smart green eyes, her snow white skin, Maggie who could sing the rage right out of the world with her sweet voice, replacing it with lightheaded ease and welcomed confusion.

During her freshman year she had her fleshy moments with boys. Usually they were clumsy, half-eaten moments. The boys were just that, boys. They poked and prodded, nibbled and teased at her places like she was puzzle. As if once they figured her out, they would reap the reward. After several laughable missteps and fumbles, Maggie poured the rest of her half-scored virginity into her music. The songs she composed--fueled by all the sensations her body had yet to feel--were both a masterpiece and a refuge.

When Maggie returned home for the summer, she held her ukulele to her body like a second set of ribs. She closed the gap with her before-college-friends and together they formed a trio: Maggie the retro, doll-faced songstress, her best friend Yula the keyboard playing, chain smoking vegan and lastly, Saul, the cello playing math major who'd lost his virginity to Yula in the 8th grade. Together they painted and photocopied posters and plastered them throughout Glory Town's small streets, its moody hallways.

***

When Abby spotted the poster in the coffee shop bulletin board announcing Maggie's local show, her face and her whole pelvic region went hot. But as she caught her reflection in window she was reminded of something one of her husband had said. He'd compared Abby to a retired race-horse, a creature once shiny and fast, who gave up speed and glamour for early comfort and undeserved softness. In her reflection, she saw thirty-six, the number of her years on this planet, distorted by the weight of those years, so that that the three and the six changed places. She'd kept a lean, boney figure most her life, but her breasts were too large for her frame, so they sagged and caused her back to curve and her shoulders to hunch forward. She'd let her hair grow uncut for years, a way to measure what the years had dealt her. Her golden brown hair lost luster and shine, and gray and white hair poked from her skull like silver shards.

That night she took scissors to her hair. As she cut closer and closer to her skull she felt her scalp breathe for the first time in years. She took henna to her hair now and the red tones warmed her skin tone. The rosewater she splashed on her face re-energized her complexion. Lastly, with a blue pencil she lined her hazel eyes, and for the first time in two decades, she saw the person she'd left behind.

Her body was her body, nothing more, nothing less. It wasn't gruesome or breathtaking, or any indication of what she had to offer. Her body held her up, enabled her to walk through the world sometimes with undesired visibility, with much more accountability than she'd ever asked for.

She skipped undergarments and went straight to her new Value Village ensemble: tight women's trousers, black and high-waisted, with wide legs that fell past her ankles. Over her breasts she wore a men's racer back tank top and over that, white pinstriped vest and a string of round, red beads. She glided her fingertip over a stem of red rouge and drew a singular line across her lips.

***

Everything about Maggie appeared effortless. From her kindness and charm to her talent and beauty, so that it seemed that the red lips and the black eyeliner were overkill. Maggie wore a vintage, cherry-print dress. She'd cut a few inches off but her hair still fell into perfect ringlets, framing her heart shaped face. Yula had all but butchered her own hair in hopes of being taken more seriously, and Saul had changed nothing. He wore lots of brown. He let the girls talk and sing. That was more than enough.

Maggie didn't drive, so it was Yula who picked her up and drove her into the guts of Glory Town to Main Street, to where all things artsy and musical were designated, even limited to. On their drive they talked about Saul and music and college and how they both wanted everything to change, everything from their breasts to their hair to politics, to their college majors. Nothing was so bad it needed changing, but their youth demanded it, like a parasite in an all too acquiescing host.

During the show Maggie surveyed her audience, found a sea of familiar faces: former teachers, old high school and middle school flames, her mother's best friend, her brother's girlfriend, even her childhood dentist. While initially it felt warm and easy, to Maggie the coziness also felt deadening. Just before Maggie's voice lost a sliver of its magic, she caught site of a bright red tuft of hair at the back of the crowd. From a distance, and without her glasses, Maggie mistook Abby for a boy, a man that is. But as the bodies of so many familiars shifted and swayed, Abby's incongruous breasts came into full view. Maggie didn't know why, but she suddenly felt embarrassed about the jar that sat in front of Yula's keyboard stand: the jar with its garish announcement of their college-kid ways, their need for sweaty handfuls of cash for things like nail polish remover, donuts and Red bull.

When Maggie and Yula sang Summertime, Maggie saw the tall, lean body belonging to the red tuft of hair swaying. A smiled curled up in Maggie's belly. This song could last forever, she thought. But the song came to an end in one long, sweeping note. The crowd dissipated but that swaying body, waving its red flag, stood by.

***

Abby stood half dizzy and flushed after the last note of music played. It wasn't until a small boy bumped her leg with his doughy elbow that Abby spun around and realized that aside from passersby she could no longer count on a curtain of warm bodies to shield her excitement, her eagerness. In fact, for the first time in a year, Abby held Maggie in her direct gaze and Maggie with her little red mouth and her curious eyes held her own.

To begin with Abby offered a wave and an ugly smile. Abby kept her lips tight, not showing her teeth and pushed her bottom lip up against her top, like an old man caught without his dentures. But even so, Maggie waved and parted her lips. Does she remember me? Does she think it's strange? Does she think I'm strange?

But before any of Abby's insecurities were to be validated or dismissed a round and commanding woman stepped between herself and Maggie. It was Maggie's mother, Catherine. Beaming with pride, Catherine barely resisted grabbing her daughter's face by her powder dusted cheeks, and Abby, though never having been a mother herself, recognized the cost of holding back in the mother's expression.

When the mother turned around, Abby could feel Catherine taking her in. Though Abby had changed her appearance drastically, though Abby had clung to shadows for several years attempting to blend in and survive the waves of gossip that once crushed her, she detected in Catherine's gaze a puzzled recognition.

"Hello," Catherine offered, her eyebrows locked in a question.

"Hello," Abby returned, "Your daughter is so talented."

"Isn't she though?" Catherine finally unlocked her eyes from Abby's disguise and returned a loving stare towards her daughter. Abby finally exhaled.

***

The mother like the jar was a sharp, unwelcome reminder of Maggie's gaudy dependence and lack of sophistication. If only she were worldly. She couldn't understand at the moment why it was that this lean, big-bosomy figure standing erect a few feet away triggered such a specific insecurity.

Yula was luckily at Maggie's rescue—quickly flocking to Catherine, offering up hugs and compliments. Saul cracked his knuckles and emptied the glass jar, counting the afternoon's bounty. As ejected as Maggie felt from her usual wealth of confidence and charisma, she still refused to cower. She returned her attention and her smile towards the Bowie-esque person before her. The tall person approached her finally, with her mother and her band-mates occupied, she finally reached out her hand to Maggie and said, "Hi, I'm Abby."

***

Abby had been married three times. Her first husband Elliot drowned while skinny-dipping with his secret lover. Abby never felt though that this was karma, or that he "got what he deserved." He was young, nineteen, and she was twenty. His belly and heart were full of mistakes waiting to be made. She thought always how tragic it was. To this day, she still exchanged Christmas cards and birthday cards with the girlfriend.

The second husband, Martin, reminded Abby a great deal of her father—cold, efficient, strong. He built a house with his huge, capable hands. Abby got pregnant twice, both times ending in miscarriage. After that, he wasn't so much cold, as he was desperate and sad. He built more rooms and he rooms swelled with their emptiness. He could not go on. Abby could. Abby left and Martin found a woman who gave him whole children, fat and perfect babies with juicy, gruesome cries.

The last was Abraham. Abraham with his broad shoulders, his easy looks, Abraham with his empty bottles and overflowing cups, Abraham with his curly laugh and his long, thick penis. Abraham who turned heads, Abraham with the electric touch, the smile that you felt in your legs and kidneys and cunt. Abraham had stirred Abby up in ways other men hadn't.

Abby was in the car when it happened. People might never forgive her for letting him drive, but Abraham knew his smooth talk, what buttery words to use, "I'm all good, believe me, believe me, I know better. Good as gold." Believe me.

She had believed. Abby believed even when the reports said that the three-year-old twins were killed in the crash. She'd believed.

That's when Abby couldn't go on. Abraham and Abby were both hospitalized, the mother and father of the twins in comas. Abraham went to prison after he recovered from his injuries. In prison he found one Jesus and lost one Abby. Abby went on without her own permission. Abby carried the dead children from the car wreck in her swollen veins. The guilt rode her and sucked the color from her skin, her hair, and her eyes.

But even guilt dies, at least, old pages of guilt. Yet new pages write themselves every day. How to kill those too?

***

Yula said, "Tell me everything."

Three weeks had passed since Abby introduced herself to Maggie after the show. Three weeks of Maggie blushing. Three weeks of Maggie biting her lip and standing on tip toes and three weeks of Catherine asking and wondering and Maggie politely but not so innocently shrugging it away.

Maggie said, "I don't know. It's interesting. I don't know what to say."

At this point Saul pressed her, "Are you a thing? Like, an item? Does your mom know?"

How could Maggie tell them everything? She wasn't sure what the "everything" was. She knew this: It started quite honestly by accident. That is, bumping into Abby downtown. Literally. Meaning, their bodies made contact each time. Bump a shoulder. Graze an elbow. Bump, bump, bump. Maggie would say, "Abby, right?" And Abby would nod, say, "Hello Maggie. Nice to see you." And Maggie's throat would grow cold but moist and she'd feel something dancing in her ribs. The accidents continued, bump, bump, bump. Until finally Abby said, "I'd like to see you. On purpose. Sometime." And Maggie said, "How about now?" And that's when the accidents slid off the table and down the street and they walked to the park and ate strawberries on the bench, Maggie in her flirty skirt, Abby in her trousers and dark eyeliner, Abby staring off past the tree-line at the water and Maggie staring at Abby and Maggie touching Abby's knee with her bare knee and Abby looking down at her naked legs, then into her eyes and finally, a kiss, and hands on thighs and then and then, and she guessed that must be the "everything" but somehow it still wasn't and she couldn't bear to give Yula that and let Yula think, 'That's it?" She couldn't bear to give her the everything that really wasn't The Everything. So she said, "I just don't know." And Yula and Paul looked at one another and then at her and said, "Whatever."

***

Abby lived in an Airstream with an old dog named Atticus. To pay bills she prepared people's taxes. She made most her income during tax season and the rest of the year did bookkeeping from her home for a handful of small businesses. Her Airstream sat on a lot belonging to a local doctor in the woods, encircled by evergreens. This was Abby's home: a collection of ties, three from each husband, except Abraham who only owned one tie which he wore to their wedding, an ashtray turned paperweight, a book of poetry by e.e. cummings, The Little Prince, and a Bible. This was also Abby's home: Service for one, a flatulent, nine-year-old Irish Wolfhound, a dog bowl, a quilt of stars, a vibrator tucked under a red pillow. This too was Abby's home: A framed picture of John Wayne, autographed. A bottle of men's aftershave. A white dress worn three times. An urn holding her father's ashes. A small CD player. Maggie's homemade CD. Dylan. Bowie. Cash. The Beatles. More Dylan. Elvis. Hendrix. More Dylan.

But when Maggie came to visit, this was Abby's home: Porcelain curves. Slender giggles. Abby's fingers running through Abby's black curls, sighs light as air but succulent and wet. This too was Abby's home: Maggie whispering, "Promise you'll come see me when I go back to school. Promise you'll keep in touch." And this: "For as long as you want me to, I will."

And again, this was Abby's home: Maggie smoothing the sheets, leaving Abby's bed sharper than before, Maggie standing in pink bra and underwear as she fluffed the pillows and stacked them. Maggie singing while she dressed. Maggie in her perfect dress leaving to make her curfew. Maggie drowning in the evergreens as she waved goodbye, Goodbye for now. Goodbye.

This was Abby's house: Abby alone but for Atticus. Abby in her wife-beater and boxers. Abby reaching for the picture between the pages once more. Abby sobbing. Abby knowing. Abby hoping. Abby asking with her hand buried deep between her legs.

***

On a Saturday night, Maggie played her last show of the summer with Yula and Saul and she could tell: They both wore sour news on their faces. Catherine had approached them earlier, they said. Catherine brought them cookies and smiles. Catherine wanted to know about the Everything that was Maggie and Abby. Yula and Saul told Catherine they knew nothing which was far from everything and Catherine had set down the plate filled with cookies and pulled out an article from her purse. It was an article about Abby printed off the internet, at least it was Abby's name they said, but it was a picture of a sad, weathered looking Abby and an story about dead children and a drunk driver. But Abby wasn't the driver, Yula chimed in, A man did it, Saul said. But that wasn't all, Yula said. Catherine told them that Abby had a dark, dark past: three marriages and the accident, and This. And that's when Catherine had pulled out another black and white page with a picture of a little boy. It was Abby but not Abby. That is, Yula started, Abby was a boy? But she said it like a question because in truth, Yula didn't know and really no one really did, and that is what she told Maggie.

But all Maggie could think about was Abby, her Abby with some bristly man. Her Abby with men. Men with clumsy penises. Men with thick necks. Men with hairy scrotum and bad breath. She did not care about accidents, or androgynous school pictures. She cared about what those bodies did with Abby's body which was now part of Maggie's body in stolen moments under a quilt and red pillow. She suddenly had the urge to pat her body in every place Abby had also touched her, as if to make sure it was all still there. But what she found was that more existed now than before. That Abby had breathed new parts into Maggie's young skin and now she was more than just Girl or Person and she felt so dizzy she began to cry. Yula and Saul each took one side of her body, trying to press comfort into her bones. But they didn't, they couldn't understand what parts needed healing and what parts just needed watering.

***

This was why Abby had let her hair grow shapeless and colorless for so many years. This was why Abby dressed like a Crone and waited for God to get down to business. This was the reason Abby lived in the woods with her friend dog. This was the reason Abby had an unlisted number. This was why Abby kept the ties close and picture closer. This was why Abby had lived like a snail. This was why: because of the Catherines, because of such bodies born with absolute sureness of gender, with no capacity to measure the pain in others less sure, and much less absolute.

Because of the Catherines.

But Maggie, she thought. Maggie she always thought. Maggie was worth it. Maggie who told Abby, "Boys have handled me like a Rubix cube. Not like you, like how you inhale me, and then when you breathe me out some parts of me are on fire and some parts are covered in goose bumps."

Yes, Abby felt the shell breaking. Yes, she knew that one Catherine could multiply into an army of Catherines and those Catherines could paint Abby's picture in blood and between her legs they would paint a sloppy dick and balls. They'd maybe paint horns on her head. They'd maybe draw a red, red circle around the misconstrued assumptions of her body and paint a bold slash over the whole mess of their composition of Abby, this stranger, this woman they did not, could not know.

But Maggie. Maggie and her soft legs. Maggie and her velvet songs. Maggie coursed through her veins, reinforced the unprotected layers, the swollen and vulnerable cracks of Abby's uniform. But were they enough to withstand the sharp edged swords of each and every Catherine in town?

Maggie had given this: Her virginity. Her songs. Her sex. Her lips. Her delicacy. Her brazenness. Her reputation. Her confidence. Abby returned what she could. Having almost twenty years on Maggie, her gifts weren't the same. Abby had courage and that courage carried her sometimes half hazardly towards Maggie, sometimes even right through her. Abby knew what she needed to give Maggie before the summer ended and it was a gift she was terrified to give. That's how Abby knew it was The One. It was her story and her story was this:

"My parents called me Archer, after my dad. They dressed me like a boy, they called me son and sometimes junior. Mom was a nurse. When I got sick it was mom that doctored me up. When I turned five and I was about to start school my parents started acting nervous. Dad bought me a fire engine the night before my first day. He told me how I could be a fireman or policeman or a president, man. 'But don't forget, you'll always be my boy,' he told me.

"I liked kindergarten. The kids were really nice and my teacher Mrs. Joyce was this sweet, tiny, pretty thing, a lot like you. She was a sweetheart. Everything was going great until the first bathroom break. I was still young enough that when I was out with my parents I'd use the ladies room with mom.

"When I pulled down my pants in front of the boys they knew I was different. They started saying, 'Hey, you're a girl! Archer's a girrrrl.'

"I got angry and yelled back and asked why they were saying that to me. This boy, I think he was named Paul, he said, 'Cause you don't have a wiener!' and another boy said, 'A penis! You don't have a penis.'

"When I got home as you can imagine, I was a complete mess and I told my parents what happened."

"What did they say? How did they try to explain it?" Maggie asked.

"They told me I was just a late bloomer, that lots of boys are late bloomers and that my penis just hadn't bloomed yet. I asked when it would happen and they just said, you'll see, it will happen. Be patient.'

"A year had passed and still no penis blooming. By then my parents had another baby and named her Shawn. The first time I saw them change her diaper I noticed she looked just like me. I asked how do they know she's not a boy, a late bloomer? But mother didn't answer, she just smiled and asked me to fetch her some baby lotion.

"That night I couldn't sleep. I heard Shawn cry and I went to her room. I had to see her, down there, I had to make sure she wasn't a boy with a late blooming penis, like me. I was only six…I didn't know.

"When my parents found me inspecting the baby's privates they hit me, then they hit me harder. They told me I was never allowed around the baby again. They called me a pervert.

"They kept me home from school for several days and then Mrs. Joyce, who thought I should do another year with her—got worried. She made a home visit and when she saw the shape I was in, well, you can imagine…I never saw them again."

"Good Good riddance!" Maggie said, face growing flushed, "I bet you were relieved."

"No, not at all. They did terrible things, but they were all I knew of family. I was petrified. Not only that but when the doctor examined me thinking I was a-six year-old boy named Archer, he just about had a heart attack and his shock just about gave me one too. An endless parade of therapists and social workers came through. A heavy set older woman with a high-pitched voice came in and started asking questions. She brought books and asked what I knew about the birds and the bees. I shrugged and said bees buzz and birds sing, both can fly and both start with the letter "B". She said I was a very smart little girl. Something about the way she said it made me cry.

"She opened the books and showed me lots of embarrassing pictures. I saw myself in some of them. She said, 'Girls have vaginas and boys have penises.' I told her that my penis just hadn't grown yet, and that I was a late bloomer.

"She said nothing back. In fact she left the room and didn't come back, even though she said she was going to. Instead a man in a suit came in. He was all serious and hollow."

***

Because Maggie was young and beautiful she was also impatient. She understood why she needed to hear all about Archer and the awful parents. But Maggie wanted, needed, to know about the husbands. She wanted to know why Abby married them and why she left them. She like so many young lovers in their first serious love affair, Maggie wanted to catalog the truancies and misdemeanors so she could avoid them, so she could be the last love of all. Maggie asked:

Did you love them?

What did you love about them?

Why did you stop loving them?

How much did you love them?

Do you miss them?

Do you love me as much as you loved them?

What if your love for me runs out?

How can you be sure?

Will you tell me?

Do you promise?

How do I know you mean it?

A quieter voice inside told Maggie to stop and listen. That same voice whispered, 'Not now, not now, shh and make love, shhh and bury your head in her lap, don't do this, please...' But that voice was too quiet and too docile to teach a girl in love anything.

***

Abby had only one answer for all of Maggie's questions. She pulled Maggie onto her back, spread her legs apart, kissed her breasts, looked into her eyes, and thrust. Maggie gave a surprised little gasp.

Abby said, "My parents were right about me. I was, I am, a late bloomer."

***

When Yula and Saul drove Maggie to the airport they didn't ask questions. Maggie knew why. For the first time in their unapologetically young lives their trio had encountered The Sacred. The thing that becomes so much The Everything that it is no longer something you can divulge on a drive to the airport or on a drive to anywhere for that matter. It wasn't the same as a secret, its roots were deeper, older. As Maggie felt the memories of Abby and the summer trickle down her throat, she also traced them on her neck as if to make sure they'd always be a part of her.

When the silence overstayed its welcome Yula began to sing We Built this City and Saul laughed and poked Yula's shoulder and Maggie could tell they'd had sex again. Saul sang too, and Maggie joined in eventually as she finally remembered what life was like before.

***

Atticus licked the tears off Abby's cheeks until she pushed him away, drying off both tears and saliva with her red pillow.

Abby added a second picture between the pages of her Little Prince book: a picture of Maggie singing, her eyes closed, her bright, white hands cradling the microphone, the summer sky framing her in the sharpest shade of blue. No one else in the photo. In the sky. In the world. No Catherines. No Abbys either. Just the girl who finally made her a man.

Pretty Girls

I'm crazy for pretty girls. Just crazy. Don't they know how pretty they are? I can't stand it! They must know, do they? God, they drive me crazy. I heard a pretty girl fart the other day but it didn't make her any less pretty. Her face turned red, well mostly her cheeks, and it smelled really bad, like rotten eggs and I thought she was going to cry. But it was just me that heard and I know pretty girls, even the prettiest of pretty girls, do things like fart and poop and what-not. She walked away fast in her green high heels from the scene of the supposed crime.

Some girls are so pretty they make my insides hurt. I can't stop looking at them. I think they think I'm a lesbian. I'm not a lesbian. At least I don't think so. But it hurts, it hurts, it hurts to look at them and take them in and see how pretty they are all over the place. It's not like I want to have sex with them. Not really. Maybe sometimes I think I want to smell their hair or sleep next them and wake up to their prettiness. Maybe sometimes I want to turn their pretty into liquid and drink it down. God what that would do to my insides!

When I was very little my sister and I cut pictures of pretty girls out of our mother's Sears Roebuck Catalog. My sister liked to cut out the girls wearing pink and floral dresses but I liked the girls in solids with long straight hair and pretty smiles. We cut those girls out and glued them onto construction paper or something that would make them last. We drew clothes for pretty paper girls and we dressed them in Crayola crayon fashion when we wanted to and didn't when we didn't feel like it. Because sometimes we just wanted the pretty girls dressed in underwear or in nighties. Sometimes we wanted them to show their pretty skin, but mostly, if I'm being honest, that was me. I wanted them like that.

Sometimes girls are so pretty I want to pull out my hair. Sometimes I want to slap their butts or punch them in the boob. But I feel scared, maybe they can tell this is what I'm thinking. Sometimes other pretty girls look at prettier girls and they say in a very hushed and kind of angry whisper that they wish they looked like her. Oh I wish I were skinny like that. I wish boys thought I was hot like that. I wish I had her hair. Her eyes. Her skin. Her life.

But I don't want to be inside those girls. I don't want that Big Pretty that makes people like me want to punch you in the tit or swallow you up or spank your ass. I don't want that kind of design on me because I think I would go nuts. It's already bad, this going mad when I see how pretty the pretty girls can really get! More than anything, pretty girls make me hungry and I think, thank god I'm not one of those girls. Because think of it, just trying to get a cup of coffee or buy a pair of shoes and all the while all the suits of flesh, all the lip licking apes and less pretty things around you, they want to devour you. Who wants to live like that?

The Message

A young woman had a son but no husband. She worked as a maid scrubbing caked mud off lobby floors. She picked up wrappers left behind by children. She carried two buckets of water at a time, up six flights of stairs. Her black hair turned white and straw-like in just a few years. The skin on her hands turned so translucent you could see the blood pulsing beneath the surface. The woman's body aged so much that passersby believed she was the boy's grandmother.

The woman worked herself into an old lady so her son could go to college. She imagined him as a doctor, a business man, a school teacher. She imagined him never immersing his hands in buckets full of Clorox Bleach and hot water. Never scraping gum from under tables, never eating slices of orange off the floor left behind by hurried crowds.

When the boy became a man the mother took out a schoolbook from many years ago that she never learned how to read. Inside, she had carved a space where she had stashed the money she'd bled for all these years.

"This is for your dreams," the mother told him, with tears in her eyes.

He grabbed a few bills from the top, to make sure they were real.

"My dream," he told her, "is to wander the world, on my own, with nothing but the shirt on my back and the hat on my head. My dream is to dig my hands in the dirt and make my own way. My dream is to walk circles around the world, until one day I find my father. Then I will rest."

The son put the bills back. He closed the book. He kissed his mother on the cheek and walked out the door.

The woman threw the cash in the stove. She collapsed and cried so hard, her tears flooded the kitchen floor. The empty book floated to the surface. The woman reached out just before going under. Her wrinkled hand fit the carved out space as if the two were made for each other. Black letters appeared on her fingers and palms, grew into sentences, then paragraphs, and lastly, pages. She still couldn't read the words. She didn't need to.

Graduation

The Doctor who fixed Maria's madness was nearly impossible to look at. Not because she was ugly, but because she was so severely handsome. Her face and body were arranged in sharp angles that sliced the air as she moved through space. When the Doctor sat in her armchair, Maria wondered if the cushions cried out when the daggers of her elbows sunk into them.

Once healed, Maria's Doctor opened her arms, revealing the barbwire bridge of veins leading to her frozen chest. As Maria approached, she noticed the Doctor's eyes for the first time, gray planets blurred by milky steam, full of memories, of things that aren't supposed to happen, but quite often do. When the Doctor's patients graduate, they say they wouldn't change a thing, wouldn't be who they are without the curling iron, the fists, the closets, the torn nylons, the china, the snow, the father, the mother, the brother the sister, at least, that's what they say.

The embrace might grant them each a gift. For Maria, this might cauterize the mended places in her mind. For the Doctor, it might offer the gift of softness that only a human touch can. Maria pressed her doughy body into the Doctor's jagged rock one.

They say that when the Doctor shattered, her cells broke into shards of stone and scattered throughout neighborhood gardens. The stones held down the roots of daffodils and tulips until the rains came and pushed them into the earth, like hard pillows for earthworms and ants.

They say the stones are still listening to whispers of damage. They say Maria kept three, the same ones she let slip away while she was still broken.

Mothers in Trees

As a young girl Lupe stole dolls from toddlers, played pranks on her little sister, and dipped her pinky into the Holy Water.

Though she wasn't beautiful Lupe was pretty enough. More than that she was smart, talented and sassy. Boys either found her to be a hard headed little witch or an utterly enchanting girl genius. Lupe valued boys who could quote Shakespeare, or Faulkner or Hemmingway, boys who knew when to capitalize, and where to put periods and semi-colons. Lupe carefully inspected love letters from would-be suitors for errors in grammar, misspellings and repetitive adjectives. She was generous with her red ink pen, crossing out obvious clichés, circling passive language. In the end she'd return the letters without a word often smoothing the stationary out before displaying it face up on a young boy's desk.

Lupe also fancied herself a spy and took it upon herself to watch the comings and goings of amorous neighbors. When she tired of spying, she took to thievery, stealing bracelets and baskets from street vendors. When spying and stealing failed to thrill her she'd find someone or something to bother and rile up. One day she decided to torture her mother's chickens. After all, she found them insignificant. They were meat on legs running and cackling obnoxiously through the dusty yard.

That day Lupe was not thinking of the nine-foot leather belt that had once belonged to her great, great grandmother Concha who they called "The Hippo." Since she could no longer fit through the door, when Concha died friends and family were forced to break down the walls of her house. It took twenty men just to lift her off the floor. But even the strongest men in the village couldn't manage to move her more than just a couple feet. According to Lupe's mother, at least two of the men had heart attacks that day from the strain the lifting put on their bodies. Rather than risk the lives and health of the rest of the men, the movers decided to bury Concha where she fell so that her home became her catacomb. They dug a huge hole through the floor, the pavement, and the dirt, rolled Concha in, and covered her up. They stuck a cross to mark her grave. They say that the cross was buried in a tropical storm and that after a while people forgot what lay beneath the mound of dirt and someone built a slide and a swing-set there.

Concha's belt became something of an urban myth. School children insisted that as it passed from mother to daughter the belt grew even longer, thicker. So when Lupe, who was chasing a flock of terrified chickens, heard the belt cutting through air she dropped the mango she had in her right hand, ready to throw at one of the slower hens. The leather hit her spine like a jagged string of teeth. Hard as she tried not to give her mother the satisfaction, she couldn't help but wail and collapse face first, where she met the hens at eye level.

"Your punishment is this," her mother started, "I'm going to the market. It shouldn't take me more than two hours. You like to terrorize these hens, Lupe, no? Pues, I have a job for you. Catch one of these," she pointed at one cluster, "and cut her head off. Then pluck the feathers off her body, cut her again and pull out all her guts. Then, you cook her. When I get home I want to see the feast on the table. ¡Para que te da pena!"

The thought of touching a dirty chicken let alone feeling its warm blood splash her face, was worse than the promise of a whipping. As soon as Lupe's mother's wide, dark figure turned its back and walked away Lupe did what she did best in moments like this. She climbed the mango tree.

It's not that the belt couldn't have reached her. It's that Lupe's mother loved that tree. Lupe had positioned herself thoughtfully so that branches strewn with mangos enveloped her at every angle. Lupe's mother didn't dare risk bruising and knocking down the mangos. Instead she would wait for a heavy rain to flush Lupe out, or hunger, or loneliness.

"This time," Lupe's mother said, "When I whip you, the belt will wrap around your arms and legs so you can never climb my tree again."

With the chicken chaser up in the tree the hens were free to "bawk-bawk" and parade around the yard without fear. That is when the rooster cut through the assembled hens like Moses parting the red sea, approaching the tree with great pomp and purpose.

It turned out, the rooster was a poet. He scratched words in the dirt that melted Lupe's milk chocolate skin. He knew the precise placement of the comma, the difference between "your" and "you're." Even his penmanship was impeccable. Lupe read his words out loud and when she did the rooster did a little dance, as though he were worshipping her.

Lupe's mother would be home in less than half an hour, and what would she find, but Lupe enamored with the literary genius of a rooster. Even with minutes to spare, Lupe imagined the belt coming at her like a skinny dragon with all its teeth on fire. But as long as she stayed in the tree, she could not know for sure if the rooster was a poet taking the form of a rooster, or a rooster posing as a poet.

Finally, Lupe decided it was time one way or the other to face her fate. She climbed down with her back to the rooster. Her smile was taking over her face and she felt no girl should flatter a rooster with such blatant adoration. She turned coquettishly and walked towards the rooster like a muse. It was because of such a state that it came as such a shock to her when she felt a sharp peck at her heel. She turned looked down and saw a testy little hen. When the rooster tilted his body to get a better look at the hen, Lupe could see she was no longer the center of his universe.

When her mother arrived home from the market, Lupe was still plucking the last feathers from the limp, headless body, her legs covered in red dust and trampled poetry.

Finding Jesus

Our neighbor Chuck named his Rottweiler Jesus to make a point. So that when proselytizers roamed our neighborhood and the rest of us closed our blinds and turned off our lights, Chuck stood out on his porch smoking and waving with Jesus at his side.

Jesus knows two tricks; how to sit, how to shake. When Jehovah's Witnesses stop by with the Watchtower and Awake magazines, Chuck says, "Look what I taught Jesus to do," and he insists they shake his paw. One time, a little girl crawled out of her mama's skirt to meet Jesus. I watched through my laundry room window. The little girl squat on the concrete steps in her pink gingham dress and took Jesus' paw into her itty-bitty hand. "Whatch'ya think of Jesus?" Chuck asked her. "I thought Jesus was white," she said, and the mother's skirt swallowed her up again.

The two Catholic families on the block insist they're false prophets. Among the rest of us home-but-hiding, like my wife Molly and me, are various other factors narrowed down to one: fear. They ask you all sorts of things that are none of their business. Like, Do you think God cares? What is your hope for the afterlife? Do you accept Jesus Christ as your Savior? But scariest of all, When can we come back to discuss this topic with you in more detail? Each time they arrive armed with a series of questions to keep you on your porch and shut the hell up. They flip through their Bibles before you can finish your sentence to show you why whatever it was you were about to say was devastatingly wrong. You tell them you're not interested, they ask you, What are you not interested in, the Bible, religion or God? Doesn't matter which one you pick. They've got a Bible page dog tagged to show you why should be interested in all three. After a while, you give up trying to defend yourself to these strangers, you stop answering the door, and you watch Chuck have at it with them, Chuck, being the kid in who once dropped ex-lax in his teacher's coffee.

The only other non-hider in the neighborhood besides Chuck is the widow Mrs. Castillo. Her son visits only on holidays and the other neighbors are afraid to make eye contact with her, being that she'll leech onto them and ask them to help her "tape her shows" or, help her find her glasses. Mrs. Castillo awaits the proselytizers of various sects with Chuck's same eagerness. She gets a home-visit from Mormon missionaries twice a week, on Tuesdays and Thursdays, and one Bible-study a week from two Jehovah's Witnesses every Wednesday morning. On Sundays, she alternates between churches. If you ask me, Mrs. Castillo is courting with disaster. I watch her like I watch Chuck, waiting for the other shoe to drop.

Mostly Jesus spends his time in idleness, on Chuck's porch. Neighborhood boys whistle for him, "Wanna play fetch?" They yell out, "Save me Jesus!" when girls are present, but Jesus never gets the joke. His most concentrated moments of existence are ironically, during those sporadic visits from preachers and missionaries, where his purpose is simply to make the statement for Chuck, that nothing is sacred.

The joke gets old. Not only because Chuck has to announce how clever he is, "You see the look on that chick's face? Shit. That's my favorite part. I tell her, hey, I found Jesus…he was eating my garbage!" He manages two belly laughs before doubling over with a smoker's cough. Jesus wagging his tale, waiting I guess, for someone to notice his food bowl is empty. It gets old because either way, those poor bastards who go to his door are in a lose-lose situation. If they have the balls to tell him how they find it offensive, oh boy, Chuck will lay into them about freedom of speech and religion and what is this country coming to and what about the separation of church and state and how dare they come unannounced and tell him what he can and can't name his dog and besides he's an atheist and have they ever considered that, that to some people the name Jesus is just a name and not some magic utterance on which all our salvation lies, don't they think they should get a clue? If they ignore his antics, Chuck never shuts up with the one-liners; "He's wagging his tail, see? Jesus loves you!" "Another pamphlet? Sure, Jesus is paper-trained!"

Next time they come around I tell them flat out, "I'm not looking for God ladies. He knows where to find me."

Molly drops one of her hair rollers and covers her mouth. That's not all I tell them. I say, "Look, I could never do what you do. Hell, you couldn't pay me to go house to house and ask strangers what they think happens to you after you die. I wouldn't have the guts to sell donuts."

"In case something changes," the older lady says— she's got pretty green eyes and a veiny neck, "here's a pamphlet."

The younger woman is already at the bottom of my steps, looking up. She crosses her arms while the veiny one presses the pamphlet into my hand.

Jesus has gone missing. Neighborhood boys on bikes have gone searching for him. Two missionaries have come by to take Mrs. Castillo to church. Chuck grinds a half smoked cigarette into the porch railing, and I can hear Nine Inch Nails blasting from the surround sound in his living room through our open laundry room window. Molly says it might snow and if I'm too hot I should take my clothes off. She shudders in her terry cloth robe.

The boys are whistling and calling out "Jesus! Jesus!" The boys are stepping off their bikes, throwing branches at the grumpy, rising creek. The boys are looking up towards Heaven, praying with clasped hands, "Please God, let it snow."

Brothers

She said that the nectarine she bit into tasted like jazz, like Friday nights. This was the last straw for Solomon. But he couldn't tell her that he stopped loving her on account of her turning everything into poetry. He couldn't tell her that he'd grown to despise her beginning with the time she likened his melting ice cream cone to the flooding of a silky moon. It was after all, Rocky Road–for Christ's sake–and he'd been sitting in the sun with her for a good hour listening to her go on and on about the sparrows, and the light and the shadows, and didn't everything have its own song, its own harmony, its own inescapable destiny? All he wanted was to eat his ice cream. But he couldn't tell her that he'd lost all passion for her because of her lyricism.

"Too bad your lips look like that I might have loved you." With that he got up, bit into a crisp, green apple and walked away, leaving the girl to her metaphors, her seamless poetry. He strolled along and as he witnessed the day, the ugly men and women, the tedious children, the skinny, barking dogs, he smiled. He attached no meaning to their existence. There they were, there it was, and that was all.

When he came home to the house he shared with his brother, Jacob, he asked for potatoes. His younger brother did all the cooking, as he never left the house. At age sixteen Jacob came home in a state of madness saying only that he'd "seen too much of the world" and was never going out again. He said if he were to go out again, he would surely drop dead—on account of the pressure of the sky on his shoulders, the cracks in the sidewalk, the endless doors and their terrible houses. So Solomon supported the two of them with his little paper route and the errands he ran for Mrs. Puckett: Mrs. Puckett who at age seventy-five, never gave up trying to seduce Solomon, Mrs. Puckett who wore her heels to bed and drank whiskey (in Earl Grey tea) in the back of Solomon's car on the way to her hair appointments. Still, what Mrs. Puckett gave paid for potatoes and cigarettes.

"I ended things with that wordy girl," Solomon announced, "I don't want a book. I want a woman."

Jacob wanted to understand his brother. He offered him more leeks. Jacob had heard of this girl for months now. Having never seen her, he had no choice but create his own portrait of her. He imagined a girl with brown curls, like his mother had before she married his angry father. He imagined her conversing in poems on a park bench, never looking in one particular direction, but always somewhere upwards, her eyes never focusing on anything tangible, anything obvious. He imagined her pages suspended in sky.

"If she comes here looking for me," Solomon told his brother, "Get rid of her."

Several weeks passed and the girl did not come. In that time Mrs. Puckett had twice tried to get Solomon to undress her, saying her arthritis was acting up, and she couldn't possibly tug at the zipper like that, her wrists would surely snap from the pressure. In that same time, Jacob had swept the floor fifty-three times, he'd cooked well over one hundred potatoes, he'd waited all day, every day, for his brother's return, a way to taste and smell the world, without letting the world taste and smell him. Jacob could never tell anyone what happened to him that one day when he was sixteen. That day, he went out, looked around, and everything he saw was skinless. That is to say, all the filters on the living had vanished. He'd become accustomed to seeing people as walking puzzles, but on that day, there was a moment when the pieces came together. No one was a mystery. That day, people were made of glass. A crumpled old man, bent down to pick up his donut—it had fallen as he juggled it with a newspaper and coffee. A goat-faced boy snatched it before the old man could reach it. He stuffed it into his mouth all at once and ran—his blue shorts a flag showcasing his ornery success. The old man sobbed openly on the sidewalk. Jacob stood close enough to hear the glass shatter.

In his celibacy and in the absence of a wordy woman, Solomon grew fond of Mrs. Puckett in unexpected ways. Maybe it was because they drank tea in silence—no commentary about what it felt like to drink the tea, mind you, just the drinking of it alone. Maybe it was because her little blue eyes disappeared when she smiled each time Solomon opened her car door, letting her out onto that same sidewalk his brother Jacob feared so fervently.

Solomon thought he'd tell Mrs. Puckett that she had finally won. But upon arriving at her door, he found that he wanted to tell her much more and what he had not counted on was the urge to give Mrs. Puckett a description of her victory, a comparison of her with something else, and he found himself lonely for that irritating girl's way with words.

Jacob was not accustomed to opening the door of his own home. But someone was knocking as if her very life depended on it. Upon opening the door, a sorry looking girl with flat brown curls, a girl who'd sewn her lips together—resembling a seam binding two quilt squares— stood before him, holding out an envelope, addressed: For Solomon. In the young girl's eyes, Jacob saw painstaking words threaded together in a sea of books and he too, felt himself drowning. The girl left Jacob to that familiar misery, and floated away, the sidewalk devouring each one of her steps.

At a loss for words, Solomon left Mrs. Puckett with daisies and an open door. He returned home to find his own door stuttering, the door not knowing which way it should swing. He noticed the envelope with his name on it. Inside, a note asked, "And now?"

"Where is she? Where is she, Jacob?" Solomon searched the house desperate for either one of them. But the house was like a vacuum and he felt the hostile air surround him with its cold fingers. In his hand, the note, the words rubbing off inside his sweaty palm.

"Jacob!"

But Jacob had walked out barefoot, ventured into that sickening street, trembling. He'd braved the open mouth of the city, hoping the girl's pages would lead the way, hoping they would carry him off his feet.

Wolf Story

Maria had a dream about a fat boy who led a parade of blind people and spry deer. She knew the boy at least, was real. Monday afternoon she'd seen him pedal his red bike past a caution sign and bright orange traffic cones. He rode with a pink frosted donut half hanging from his mouth.

The next morning on her drive to work she stopped her car for a skinny wolf trying to cross the street. Previous cars weren't so thoughtful and the young wolf had been waiting all morning, growing hungrier for the stillness only she gave him. The wolf lurked as far as the start of the pavement, beyond the edge of the woods. He sat and smiled towards Maria.

Maria took this as an invitation and started to call him.

"Here boy," she guessed, "Come here."

Without even bothering to check the time, or concern herself with getting to the office, Maria opened her car door and whistled for the wolf to come inside.

Being young and without the necessary doubts that age and wisdom bring, the young wolf's hunger lulled him inside. He climbed onto the passenger seat, panting happily.

Inside her apartment, Maria dropped her keys into a bowl and removed her shoes without using her hands, only the heels and toes of her feet. She patted her thigh and gave a sharp, short whistle to let the wolf know, he was safe. The wolf abandoned all timidity at the scent of burnt toast and coffee. He trotted quickly into Maria's kitchen and stood on his hind legs, his paws on the counter, sniffing the toaster.

"You must be starved!" Maria said, "Maybe I interrupted your hunt. Whatever is mine is yours."

She offered a bran muffin. He politely declined, pushing it away with his black nose.

"Of course, not," she put her finger to her frowning lips.

Maria carefully considered the contents of her fridge, eggs, sausage, beans, yogurt, and apple cider. She offered a buffet style meal spread out the kitchen tile floor. But although she could hear the grumbling in the wolf's belly, he showed no interest in any of it.

Maria remembered something she read long ago, that to make peace with a wild thing you must offer them a gift, a living gift. And what other living thing did she have to offer but herself? It wouldn't be the first time, she thought, and so like she had so many other times in her life, she undressed. She stripped down to a pink bra and underwear. She laid herself out on the kitchen floor and closed her eyes.

The wolf tilted his head side to side, trying to make sense of her offering. Finally, he crawled over to her, hesitantly but with purpose.

He started with her toes, sniffing and licking, then her knees and the curve of her hip. He stopped at her navel and put his hear to her belly to listen, as though that's where her heart lived.

"Do you love me to the moon?" she asked, her eyes still closed.

But the wolf backed away from her.

"Do you love me to the sky?"

The wolf groaned and shook his head.

"Do you love me to the ceiling?"

Finally, the young wolf crept from her belly to her face, running his nose along her forehead.

"To the ceiling then? To the ceiling is pretty good."

In that moment of satisfaction, Maria's naked skin became like the earth beneath the forest, emitting the scent of every kind of prey, from fatty to dense, from those with wings, to those with hooves. Maria's body had become each and everyone inside that answer.

The wolf started with her hair, which smelled like sick deer and wet leaves. He ate every strand and he was filled up.

Maria kept her eyes shut, her cool and unencumbered scalp new and sweet. She stroked the skin below her bellybutton.

"Right here," she said. "Put your head here."

Maria took both her palms, put them behind his ears, and massaged them with her thumb and forefinger. The wolf hummed a low hum, one like the static off the T.V., the vibration of the refrigerator.

But shortly after his "meal", the wolf began to moan. It was clear he was aching, maybe even dying. Maria sat up in a hurry, and put her hand to his arched back. She watched him heave and heave until he vomited a cocoon made of her hair.

"Poor thing, what have I done!"

She curled her naked torso closer to his weak body; with one hand still on his back she laid her other hand on his belly. The dry heaves continued, followed by a bowel-anchored howl. Maria watched as the wolf's throat engorged until finally he coughed up the culprit—a pair of red handlebars. The spent wolf trembled and fell to the floor.

"The boy?" Maria asked, "The boy on the red bike?"

But the wolf didn't answer. He only moaned.

"You ate the boy! You killed the boy on my bike! The boy from my dream!"

Maria yelled, pulling away from him.

But the wolf, looking even slighter than before, tried to crawl to her his front paws scooting towards her naked lap.

"This always happens to me! Why me?"

With that she grabbed her clothes and cursed the wolf a few more times.

Maria wrapped herself in her hair cocoon concealing her contours and curves. She left the wolf the apartment, keys, and car. Barefoot she seemed to float into the nearby woods. Half a mile from her home Maria found the place where houses and streets vanish and only trunks and leaves remain. The sky's pale-blue fabric, an expanding roof ready to cave.

Meanwhile on a hidden street beyond the edge of the woods, a fat-faced boy parades his shiny new yellow bike, sterling compensation for his scraped knees, his slight bruises.

The Guppy Suicides

Maggie was still in pigtails and pampers when her guppies leapt out of the fishbowl. On the carpet they looked nothing like fish but more like specks of fabric. She squished them with her naked heel then confessed to her mother who told her that such little things are temporary anyway.

She was only two years older when she asked her father to kill the mouse she'd found in her toy box. She had tried herself. To step on it would have made a mess so Maggie tried Saran Wrap, but the mouse kept breathing. She dropped the scurrying mouse in a jar and handed it to her father. Maggie watched to see how he would deal with it. He broke a branch off the apple tree and stabbed the mouse until the glass went red then he tossed the jar into dumpster and threw the branch to the curb.

Maggie was nine when she noticed the bird didn't fly away no matter how close she got. She bent over to pick it up and it opened its beak. Maggie dipped her finger in the bird bath and let a drop fall into the bird's mouth. Her mother said, "Don't touch that, it's dirty." So Maggie hid the bird inside of her dress and snuck her into her bedroom.

The bird would not eat or drink. Its chest rose and fell. Maggie waited. No song came. No chirping, only the struggle to breathe.

When the bird died in Maggie's trembling palms, she took a ceramic bowl from her mother's cabinet and a roll of paper towels. She wrapped the dead bird in some towels and placed it in the center of the bowl. Maggie buried the bird inside its casket bowl in the very back corner of the yard, beyond the strawberries and lettuce. She drove a stake into the loose dirt to mark the grave.

A week later, Maggie wondered if she'd been wrong about the bird. The dirt was still loose enough she could dig with her hands. She felt the bowl and lifted it out of the hole. The small mass inside the paper towel was still soft. She unraveled the paper towel. Yellow goo fused the bird to the paper. Maggie held her breath, wrapped the bird up again, stuck it in the bowl, and pushed the dirt back on top. She threw the stake over the fence.

Some goo and a small feather stuck to the end of Maggie's forefinger. She couldn't shake it off. She passed some daisies, knelt down, and rubbed the petals to peel the feather off. A bee buzzed near her arm, and Maggie felt the sting. The red mark on her arm began to swell. But Maggie told no one.

The Sisters

Big Sister walked and Little Sister floated. What passerby saw was a scowling, lanky girl dressed in blue dragging a limp, white, kite behind her. Little Sister wore white on account of Mother telling her she was a gift from Heaven.

Big Sister grew sick of how Mother would ask Little Sister, "Why are you so, so sweet? How does it come so easy for you to be such an angel?" Big Sister became incensed with Little Sister's dim-witted smile, and the horrible sound of the wet kisses Little Sister would plant Mother's cheek.

On one of their walks Big Sister pointed out a dead blue jay in the street's gutter. The bird's chest had deflated like a squashed peach. The eyes hollowed out, the legs bent and twisted so they resembled question marks.

"See that?" Big Sister pointed, "Heaven is filled with them. Hundreds and thousands of things just like that."

Little Sister let go of Big Sister's hand. To passersby it appeared as though the breeze had abandoned the kite, leaving it lost in its awkward back and forth dance.

When Mother died someone stuffed her into a coffin, dressed her in a green and black floral print polyester dress. This was not Mother's loveliest dress by any stretch of the imagination. But someone had decided it was. Someone had also decided Mother looked too dead for her own funeral and had painted her face with dark rouge, so that Mother resembled a frightening, mad, old woman.

Looking at Mother inside that rectangle box Little Sister remembered Big Sister's words from years before. "Heaven is filled with them."

The Sisters hosted the wake like parallel statues never turning to look at one another until finally, Big Sister cut off a piece of pink frosted cake and offered it to Little Sister, to which she shook her head, No.

The Sisters old ladies now live on opposite sides of the same town and every time they meet on the street Big Sister says, "Hello. How are you?" Little Sister says, "Very well." "That's good," says Big Sister and Little Sister walks away.

The next time they meet Big Sister says, "Hello. How are you?" Little Sister responds the same as usual. But this time Big Sister says, "Why have you never asked me, 'How are you?' In all these years…"

"Haven't I? I thought I had."

Little Sister looks down at the oil in the gutter, she watches the swirls of green and blue, how they curve around one another without ever touching.

Birth

A woman was in the habit of taking on lovers and not repeating herself. At night, upon their arrival she would open the door to her home without a word, turn and walk away, letting her silky cape fall to the floor, leaving a trail for the man in the doorway. In the dark, her body was a collection of moons. In the morning she would offer coffee, and leave all conversation to her paramour, while keeping herself in little books, secretly stacked inside her ribs.

One lover wanted the library of her. This was a tricky business. He had to fool her with countless disguises so she wouldn't tire of him. Every time he came to her, he was a new man. He paid attention to what endeared her to his many faces, until he knew how to put them together into one man. One night, he decided his collage was complete, and while she slept, he cut out a diamond-shaped piece of her skin below her belly button. He ate the flesh to keep part of her inside of him, assuming this was the way.

When she awoke, he told her, "There will be no more others." She smiled, because in truth, this woman wanted someone to put an end to her dizzying, addictive lust.

The man could see in the woman's eyes her catalog of lovers, years of men who shared her bed, her body, and it drove him mad. He set her bed on fire. That's how it started. He would say, "Show me where else they've been in your house."

She pointed to the couch, the kitchen counter, the hallway, and the oval-shaped rug now pale and weary from the friction of bodies. She touched the bookshelves, the windowsills, the shower, the garden, the table, and the chairs surrounding the table. "Here, here, here."

"The whole house then," he said, and lit the match.

The house burned like paper, its flaming edges floating up to the sky like the ghosts of old women. Even her black cape disappeared in the smoke.

This, however, was not enough. The man demanded to know every place on her body she'd ever been touched. She surrendered to his examination. He left her naked on the grass and returned with pen and ink to mark every part of her with his name. If the ink smeared, he traced his name over and over again, each time pressing harder.

Weeks later the woman felt a shy, low trembling inside of her and announced it to the man. She likened it to dancing moths.

He kept the woman in a tree after this, so no one else could reach her. He brought her peaches and raisins, sometimes biscuits. Every night he slept at the bottom of the tree, resting upon its trunk. Some nights, he dreamt the woman grew wings, and this terrified him. In the morning, he would look up at her skinny brown arms and feel at peace again.

As the woman's belly grew, the man saw the places where he'd written his name grow as well. How big a part of her he'd become. When it came time for the child to be born the man took the woman to the beach. He promised a bed in the middle of the ocean, a cradle made from pearl, shark meat and clams for dinner, promised sealskin, cut and sewn to her flesh, where a part of her was missing.

The woman only half listened. With every contraction, her body became less and less hers, more belonging to the earth, more to the tree which had been her home for all those months. She looked down at her spread legs, and thought she saw beastly branches and coarse leaves. She closed her eyes and thought about her silky black cape, the last garment of her old life. She remembered its ashes floating on the sky like blackened moths and somehow the pain produced by this memory dulled the pain of the bearing down, the tremendous pressure.

As the woman howled, the man grew sick with anticipation, anxious to see his face atop a small, slippery body. Instead, what emerged from his round house of a woman was a full-grown, naked man, the first of many past lovers she was yet to give birth to. The woman shook her head. She dug her hands in the sand, deep, as if searching for an explanation that didn't exist.

"Whore," he said, and left her screaming, left her to her hairy, clumsy children.

The man had walked several miles before he felt the tiny explosions going off inside him, and how he regretted the part of her he'd swallowed, the diamond of her body he could not give back.

Rings

She bought the pen for her lover, not her husband. The journal also, but the journal she could replace. The pen she could not. The pen had been engraved. The husband had thought nothing of it, the poem by W.S. Merwin, "Your absence has gone through me/Like thread through a needle. /Everything I do is stitched with its color." She thought, At least he is dumb. Then later, Too bad he is dumb. The poem was titled "Separation" and life and love had separated her from her beloved, not her husband. The husband had the pen. The beloved lover did not.

The husband used the journal and pen for to-do-lists of which he was a master. He tore out pages that were never meant to be torn. The wife felt every tear pierce her very womb. Little sighs escaped her at times. The lover would know not to tear the pages; the lover would know not to stick the end of the pen in his sloppy mouth. The lover did not have a sloppy mouth. Instead it gently drew her lips in, so she could feel the gentle nudging of his teeth.

Maybe I will kill myself she thought. Or maybe I should kill him. Or maybe I should kill us both. But instead the wife cut tomatoes and lettuce. She roasted onions with garlic. She sucked in her womb, tight and miserable.

The husband said how the days were getting shorter and how the dark came sooner, much sooner than the year before and the wife could only say, Yes, I agree. And she did.

When he stood up from his recliner and picked the coffee cup from the end table the wife noticed he'd left a ring. She rinsed a sponged and squeezed off the excess water. But the husband took it from her hand without a word and washed the ring off. She said, Dinner will be ready in twenty. He said, Okay, time for a shower. He kissed her cheek, and she imagined another brown ring on her face, the smell of burnt coffee on her pretty skin.

The wife gathered the onion skins, opened the cabinet under the sink to toss them in the garbage when she noticed a few crumpled up pages from what should have been her lover's journal. She set the cutting board covered with onion skins aside on the counter. When she heard the shower turn on, she began to pick through receipts and wrappers, scavenging for the white paper blossoms. Carefully, she separated them, unfolded them, picked cereal and tea bags off each page and flattened them on the tiled floor. These were not checked off to do lists. The wife's eyes burned.

One page read: How could you?

The other read: He won't take care of you. I know how to take care of you.

And the last crinkled, tea stained page read, When I see you in the kitchen cooking me dinner I want to change. I think, this is everything. I am happy.

The wife picked the sheets up and pressed them to breast of her apron. She walked to the living room still listening to the water running upstairs. She sat in recliner and it was still warm from his body. She laid the pages on her lap letting her arms fall weakly. Across from her hung a mirror they'd once purchased at a garage sale. In the mirror she could see the kitchen. In the mirror she could see the onion skins, the shiny body of the fridge, the coffee maker and the yellow sponge on the counter. But when her husband sat, he could only see her.

She set the pages aside and rose from the chair. She walked towards the mirror and turned her face to see her cheek where instead of an ugly brown ring she saw a sparkling, pink star. She closed her eyes. Before the first tear could reach her neck, she felt his damp hand on her shoulder. When she opened her eyes and looked into the mirror once more there stood her husband right behind her, yes, but beside her, too.

The Need

She wasn't madly in love anymore, she was just mad. She wondered what would happen if she stopped acting like a wife to her husband. That is if she quit offering up the pleasing, wifely things that he'd grown accustomed to. If she stopped asking him how his day was, if she stopped picking up his dirty socks, if she stopped offering up her crotch like a dinner roll.

Her husband had bought her an aquarium on their first wedding anniversary on account of her love of fish and the sea. Because of the fish she was able to hold onto her love for him a little while more. But three years had passed. She still loved the fish but she tolerated her husband.

She wasn't sure why it was that it would always wear off. She'd fall in love like a trapeze artist and within weeks or months an unseen force stole away the passion right from under her skin and no Amber Alert could ever bring it back. The touch that once excited her and set her blood on fire now turned her guts into reckless and heavy knots. She could barely keep her coffee down when he climbed on top of her.

She thought about quitting being a wife every day until the thoughts consumed her completely. Occasionally her husband would ask if something was the matter, but she shut him up with one type of dinner roll or another. When her husband left for the day, she sat in front of her aquarium and told the fish her troubles. Garish fish eyes stunned by her attention glared back. Sometimes she dipped her fingertips in the water and some of the braver fish nibbled at her flesh. She liked it so much she started dipping her whole hand in the water. She kept her hand and her fingers very still and when a bolder fish swam close enough she'd try to close her fingers around his wiggly body. Then she'd let go. She did this several times a day, to the point of forgetting sometimes how mad she was. Water had this effect on her.

One day her husband came home and found her kneeling on a stool she'd set up next to the aquarium. She had leaned as far as she could into the aquarium until her head was submerged.

Her husband dropped his briefcase and lunchbox and screamed, "'Whatthehellareyoudoing!?" She couldn't hear him with her face plunged into the murky water. But she could see his face reddening, his fists clenched. Before he could touch her she raised her head out the water and didn't say a word. She dragged the stool away from the aquarium and placed it back at the bar in the kitchen where it belonged.

That night, he climbed on top of her again wanting her to look at him, but she could not.

"Let's fill the tub," she suggested. She filled the tub and climbed inside. But when plunged his massive feet into the water began to overflow and flood the bathroom. She started to get up but he said, No, no, Don't worry about that now. But she did worry. His entrance was graceless and clumsy. Not like a fish. There was no tender nibbling. Instead he approached her like a tsunami and his passion just about drowned her.

When she came up for air her husband was already stepping out of the tub. He walked thick and sopping across the flooded floor and collapsed onto their bad, falling fast asleep. The water had turned cold and she began to cry and shake. Some of her husband's pubic hairs rose to the surface and she cried even harder. Still naked and trembling, she drained the water until the tub was empty and shuffled her way to the kitchen to retrieve a pitcher. She used the pitcher to gather up fish and aquarium water to refill the tub. She could not risk shocking the fish to death with the temperature of the bathwater. She made several trips back and forth from the aquarium to the bathtub until the aquarium was completely empty of both fish and water. By the last trip she was no longer wet, and her goose bumps had faded. Ever so slowly, she descended into the tub where her fish swam freely in their own waste-ridden water.

She laid back and spread her legs apart, resting one foot on either corner of the tub. The smell of the water reminded her of the beach at low tide and of her first period. It was putrid and sweet. Her fish company scattered in different directions. The tetras tickled the inside of her floating arms, while the goldfish blew bubbles in her tangled hair. The cichlids swam between her legs, dug gently into her fleshy cave. She fell asleep to a wave of spasms in her womb that left her face flushed and warm.

In the morning her husband found her in the tub with all the fish and it turned his stomach so much to see the filth in the water clinging to his wife's breasts and face and hair that he vomited and the retching woke her up. Before he could say a word she told him, "We need a bigger aquarium."

To her surprise he said, "Yes, sure, I'll buy you the biggest aquarium I can find, just don't ever do that again."

"I won't empty the aquarium in here ever again if you find me a much bigger aquarium. I promise."

"Okay," he nodded, "I'll get you what you need."

She rose from the water feeling changed, not in the way of a new convert, but in the way that one does after one knows death for the first time. The way in which one nods at a funeral and says, "Yes, I've lost a loved one too, quite recently." She was now one of those people who knew about death, who could talk about it if she had to, could comfort devastated widows if she wanted to. Some pieces of waste slipped off of her, but the algae clung on. Two goldfish were tangled in her hair as she climbed out and one hit the bathroom floor and started his flipping and flopping. Casually she reached down and returned him to the water before reaching into her cold matted hair to retrieve his partner.

"You must be freezing!" her husband said touching her cheek. But she was very warm.

Standing naked before him, her flat nipples like little pink buttons, she asked, "Do you promise you will get me that big aquarium? I mean huge. Huge."

He nodded and reached for her breasts, surprised at the heat of their temperature. Water dripped from her vagina and a small cichlid slid down her leg. Her husband didn't notice.

When he left for work she didn't bother to clean the vomit in or around the toilet.

What she did was refill the aquarium. What she did was carry each fish comrade safely back home. What she did was shower and to scour her deadened skin as if to find another layer. What she did was close her eyes and imagine scrubbing off her skin and finding fish scales instead. What she did was smile and touch herself as she thought of the fish and water between her legs and dripping off her breasts. What she did was cry when she opened her eyes and found she'd rubbed her still human layer red and raw.

What she didn't do was make dinner. What she didn't do was put on make-up and panty hose. What she didn't do was make the bed or wash the dishes. What she didn't do was eat or drink or talk for the day. What she knew was this: she was dead inside of a live body.

When her husband came home that night he said, "I have something for you---"

And she felt some of that horny blood fire for him, until he opened the door wider and revealed a boyish girl in cords with wide shoulders and short blond hair and he said, "You have help now." And he sent the boyish girl make the bed and to make the dinner and to wash the sheets and even to feed the fish which was the last straw.

"That's not an aquarium," was all she could say.

He promised her soon the aquarium would come, that he had to special order it.

"That way, and until then," he told his wife, "Everything still gets done like before."

Chore by chore, the boyish girl had erased the need-to-be-done-things from their home.

So she did what she had to do. While the boyish girl busied herself scrubbing caked vomit off the bathroom tile, the wife emptied the aquarium into her tub and lay back inside with all the fish. The water was much clearer, cleaner. Honestly, it wasn't the same without that smell.

The boyish girl said, "You must really love fish," and the boyish girl raised her eyebrows, and the boyish girl was definitely not wearing a bra though the boyish girl had not much breasts anyway which is why she was a boyish girl to begin with. And the boyish girl kept smiling even as the scent of dried vomit and fishy water filled the room, even as her question went unanswered, the boyish girl smiled with her mouth, her cheeks, her eyes, she even smiled with her legs. The smile filled up the bathroom and even the fish and the warm-blooded woman among them felt the wake of the boyish girl's smile in their exclusive water.

"I wanted an aquarium. A giant aquarium. Not a person. There are already so many people."

She finally answered the boyish girl this way, and the boyish girl beamed even brighter.

"I like that," the boyish girl said.

Just then the husband reappeared having just finished the dinner cooked by the boyish girl, with a bit of gin on his breath, loosening his tie, while his pants tightened over the full, hard member between his legs. He asked the boyish girl to leave the bathroom, to clean the kitchen and the table, to clean the counters and wash the dishes and to make his lunch for tomorrow and the boyish girl's smile locked on her face into something rigid and unsettling.

"You promised," the husband said.

"So did you," said his wife, and she closed her eyes but the tears came all the same.

That night, the wife dreamed a cruel kind of dream, because it gave her what she wanted and what she did not have. She dreamed that when she woke she was a lady fish, not something as obvious as a mermaid mind you, but a lady fish. She still had all her same body parts, her chubby vagina, her little apple breasts. But she was covered in iridescent scales. The house itself was her aquarium and she could know the fish's thoughts and they could know hers, sometimes her husband knocked on the glass of their aquarium home to get her attention, but mostly he didn't. And the spaces between her and the fish took on the shape and movement of the boyish girl's smile and the smile carried them and exhausted them all at once. The smile lived sometimes inside those shapes between them, and sometimes inside them where the breathing happened. All in all, it was a beautifully wicked vision and when she woke she wondered how the dead could still dream.

The Harvest

At age fifty, after three decades of rejection, Eldon marries an onion. Before the onion, Eldon had fallen in love with hundreds of women. They were always young, slender, and charming. The first woman he ever proposed to was named Lita, she had red hair and wore a pointy bra under pink angora. He said to her, "Lita, I love you. I want to marry you." To which Lita responded, "That's nice." He was twenty then. His sisters told him it was because he kept going for young and beautiful, and young and beautiful only want rich and richer.

Eldon picks apples and pears and sometimes cherries. He takes home the bruised apples and pears that cannot be sold. He saves boxes of them for winter. He carves apples into little half-moon shavings for dessert. Eldon believes that one day, a beautiful woman will love him because he's a hardworking, honest man. He believes this woman will listen to A.M. radio in the evenings with him, eat apples with him, and that life will be simple and good.

Eldon begins wearing hats because he thinks it will make him look sophisticated, distinguished and that women will like it. It works at first. When his face is shaven and his clothes are clean, Eldon doesn't look so bad, and with a hat putting on just the right amount of shadow over his eyes, well, he's damn attractive. At least, this is what Kathy and her friend Vivian think, as they watch him walk through the park, picking cherries from a paper bag, and popping them in his mouth. The two girls ask Eldon to drive them to places. Once, even to Montana to visit Vivian's diabetic aunt. But when Eldon tries to kiss Vivian-he put his hand to her face right before-Vivian steps back, she asks to be taken home.

These scenarios continue into Eldon's thirties, and forties. Apples turn into applesauce. Eldon's hats begin to slump like sad little mushrooms. Finally he leaves apple orchards for the onion fields. He desires something less sweet. When the onions stop growing they lose their color, weaken at the top of the bulb and flop over. Less experienced gardeners ask, "What's wrong?" Not Eldon. He knows this is Nature's plan. The leaves have put the last of their energy into the bulbs. Eldon also knows that there is no wrong time to pull an onion, as onions always have something to offer.

Eldon brings home the surplus. When he chops onions into cubes for soup he doesn't fall for the sting. His eyes do not well up with tears. But as he pulls the last onion, removes her brown, papery skin, he reveals a luminous, pearly white face. Her eyes search her new surroundings. Eldon runs his finger down the side of her face. She doesn't complain about the coarseness of his hands. Take me, her eyes say.

Eldon does just that. He says his vows and takes her to bed. He points out the window at the night sky and tells her the stars are hers. He kisses her tiny mouth. They fall to sleep in purrs.

Eldon is sixty. He keeps his wife inside his hat. In the evenings, he puts her in his lap. For dinner, always soup and tea. But this night stirs with the unexpected and Eldon sets his wife on the counter and answers the door. A woman in rags stands before him, her head bowed, her feet bare.

"Can I help you?" Eldon asks.

She lifts her eyes, just barely, and says, "I was young then. I didn't know."

Eldon recognizes Vivian beneath the sun-damaged skin, the faded gray color of her eyes.

Vivian presses Eldon's hand to her cheek. "Take me," she says.

Meanwhile, Eldon's onion-wife rolls off the counter, splitting into perfect, half-moons.

The Hunchback Shops at Safeway

What if I'm wrong about the hunchback I saw in Safeway? What if he has more friends than I do? What if he sits at the dinner table every night with a wife and child, or even children? But I don't think so. I don't think so because of how his back erases his neck. I don't think so because he holds in his twisted hands a basket full of meals for one.

I think I might love the hunchback. I don't call him "The Hunchback" because I'm awful or something. I call him the hunchback because I don't know his name, or his age, or even his sign. I've seen him every week for the past five years and each time he is walking in his buttoned up plaid shirt, his suspenders that pull the waist of his pants close to his chest, his socks showing above his shoes. When I see him he is either coming or going, sometimes he is smiling a little. Each time I get this sick feeling that I want to protect him. Maybe people say evil things to him. Maybe he is very lonely. Maybe he hurts inside. Maybe I could be his friend. But I also think how awful it would be if someday he asked, "Why did you want to be my friend so long ago?" and I'd have to explain, "Because you are a hunchback, and your big head, and your high-waisted pants make you look like something unreal and because I thought you were beautiful in your strangeness, because I wanted to protect you because I worried the world had always been terrible to you and I wanted you not to be alone because I was so sure you were alone, and hurting and weary of the cruelty of mankind."

He would see this as pity and me as pitiful and he would say, "That is the cruelest thing of all." And even when I'd tell him, "No, no, it's not like that. You see, you look on the outside how I feel on the inside: strange and tangled and not quite real. Because you see, I have all the same parts as other humans but my parts are askew, my parts are dangerous and unpredictable...you see, you see..."

But he would no longer be listening. Then I would be the lonely one because I'd have lost the mirror of his face and his deformities, that which I found mythical and pure, those that I wanted to trace with my fingers as much as with my own heart, even if that sounds naive and sentimental, I did, I really did. I still do.

Luz

That morning at the first signal of rusty blood, Lucinda decided she wouldn't bleed again. She knew at that moment she absolutely, positively, without a doubt in the world must become pregnant, must give birth, must become a mother. And although she had no home and no man to call a home, even though she had no self to self-improve, even though Lucinda was weightless, really, kind of floating in the world, she believed she had to fill her womb immediately. In fact, the hunger in her womb was so deep and desperate it took over her whole body. The hunger in her belly felt petty. The emptiness of her womb gnawed at her, it growled, it begged, FEED ME!

Because Lucinda couldn't breathe on her own she carried an oxygen mask to wear around the city. With the mask pressed over her mouth and wearing the thin veil of a pillow case turned dress Lucinda went out to find someone to fill her restless womb. She didn't find one or two but twenty. She laid with each one, quietly, without warmth, without pleasure, but with hunger, always deep and non-abating hunger. All the time, she kept the mask over her face. Once she was sure the deed had been done, Lucinda went in search of a cave in which to hibernate and just wait for everything to happen to her that was going to happen. Maybe she would die of starvation or from lack of oxygen. Maybe she'd be discovered breathless and bloated in her pillowcase dress. It could end that way. She hoped, instead she'd find a place that could hold her. After all, she didn't take up much space at all. She required little. Maybe, she even required nothing, except the air she drank from her plastic mask.

Lucinda found a hole and climbed down the hole with her mask and her oxygen. She'd become accustomed to the dark, and to the wet pressure of the dirt walls. Life was joyless, but it was life. She was breathing after all. As her belly swelled larger and larger over the next nine months, climbing in and out of the hole became a chore. So when the days grew close to delivery, she grabbed all the air she could, along with some tea and soda and went down into the hole for good. She would deliver that which would finally complete her and bring her joy in the bowels of an angry park where there were no children, only more joyless survivors kicking garbage cans and yelling at trees.

One morning Lucinda looked up at the light from the bottom of the hole and knew it was time. She felt the first contraction, not just inside her body, but also around her, squeezing her. When it was time, she pushed, all the time with her mask pressed up to her face so tight it was like second skin, a secondary feature of misery. But when Lucinda pushed, it wasn't just the life inside her that moved, it was the walls around her, and though she couldn't be certain with all the delirious pain, she believed the light was getting bigger and brighter, and that she too was being pushed up and out of the hole with every contraction, with every push.

Finally, Lucinda reached the terrifying stage of labor that would either bear great fruits or rip her in two and destroy her; the Ring of Fire, the last effort to meet with either life or death. But just as she prepared to bear down for the last time, the mask fell from her face and when she tried desperately to reach for it, she noticed that her arms, her shoulders, were pinned inside the hole in the earth, and that the walls of dirt and rock had indeed all but swallowed her whole. She moved her toes, and there was no ground beneath her. She looked up and the light was white, blinding, pulsing…She tried to breathe, but the walls around her contracted, squeezing her so hard she thought her bones were breaking, stealing whatever oxygen she had left. As she took her last breath, the light emerged at its fullest and most invasive, and in an instance, all turned to black.

The first cry filled Lucinda's lungs, turned her wet, muddied, skin pink, and her pillow case dress peeled off like expired skin. Each breath filled her belly, set her cells on fire. The white room was filled with lights, little mechanical torches, cold instruments, and voices. One voice she heard more clearly than any other. A word tiptoed across her tongue. But no language could lose itself from Lucinda's throat, only a cry, the desperate and pitiful cry of a newborn child was set free. Second by second, Lucinda was forgetting. Forgetting where she'd been, forgetting her age, her illnesses, her fears, her memories no matter how traumatic or powerful or obvious. She kept on forgetting until she even forgot her name, her descent into the dark hole, the park, the mask, the oxygen, the suffocating. The forgetting calmed her cries, and the soft, clear voice guided her, pressed Lucinda's tiny mouth to her mother's breast and fed her, her first taste of freedom.

Crown

I held you in my arms after washing my hands in hot water and ivory soap for sixty seconds. That was the rule. At age eight, I believed myself an expert on how to hold new things, an expert of how to live in this noisy world. I smelled the top of your head, examined your frail fingernails. I gently flexed them, alarmed at how pliable they were. I tested mine: stiff, inflexible...already. I marveled at your softness, your absolute perfection.

When I was thirteen, I was more of an expert, and your parents asked, Can you keep your eyes on him please? And I did. You pouted, you stomped your foot while your parents busied themselves cleaning out their most recent rental, the third in one year. When I tried to take your hand in mine, an offering of comfort, you bit me. But I didn't tell. I understood it was your protest, the last straw of your patience as you watched your toys sorted, divided into labeled boxes, your clothes folded and lowered into ballooning duffel bags and plastic bins. I added the bite to my crown, a gem of my growing expertise on how to be.

When I was twenty, my crown heavy with dull rocks and broken stones, I watched you, together with my two-year-old son. You were playing with your train set, a birthday gift from your grandmother. My son stomped on the train, pulled pieces from the track, broke them in two, in three, even four, after ruthlessly chewing them up. You sat on the floor, looking at the wake of destruction my angry toddler left behind. I waited for your rage, the five-year-old who stomped his feet, who showed his teeth. But you didn't. Instead, you lifted your head, your glossy eyes questioning mine. I asked, Can it be fixed? You shook your head. No, you answered, But everything breaks, eventually. You said, You just have to let it go once it's broken. Everything breaks, I repeated.

I was twenty-eight the next time we met and you were a man, towering over the shattered pieces of my crown. I was no expert on how to live. I had only taken too long to believe it. How many years has it been? I asked, knowing full well eight years had passed. Too many, you answered. My son still talks about you, I said. You hugged me, pressing the back of my head towards you, pulling my face into your chest. I drowned in your scent. I thought, This is what I've been waiting for. This. Nothing else.

It wasn't perfect the first time, or the second. Our first kiss flooded as November poured through a canopy of evergreens. You wiped my face with the inside of your coat, as if you'd forgotten it hadn't stopped raining. My face wouldn't stay dry and not only because of the rain.

You left. To find yourself, you said, to know yourself. You were just a kid who thought he was a man, you told me. You were still growing. You were only twenty when you talked about forever. You were no expert on how to be. Be angry, tell me how horrible I am for doing this to you, you begged. I rubbed the place on my left hand, the meaty part of my thumb where you'd taken a bite out of me so long ago. I told you, Everything breaks, eventually. You left me while I sat in the tub, my skin going up in flames. I wanted the scalding water to burn the flesh right off my bones, to rid me of tissue, of nerves, anything capable of drinking and retaining this pain. White bones, a ladder of broken steps to a broken heart.

I swear it's not too late. A place must exist where broken things are made whole again, where time exists windowless, insulating this tiny kingdom. I swear it's not too late, to cure the brokenness, to heal such subtle but profound damage. I swear it isn't too late to find yourself inside this room, with me. It's not too late, I say to you, when you come back to gather your things; a guitar, a presumably lost jersey, your bags of shirts stuffed inside Safeway bags. I tell you, I kept the pieces all these years, promised myself I'd fix the track, that I'd replace the joints between the train cars. I said, I know it's a long time coming, but broken things can be fixed.

But you left.

Night after night without you, the ages between us fight their bloody wars. I have loved you in every way, maybe even with a new love that never existed before me and you. Tell me it's not too late to put down our swords. Tell me it's not too late and I will believe you. I will sink into that ruthless dream. I will wait.

But you left.

I told you I would put this pain on paper. I told you I would bear it. This is me, my love, bearing it.

The Goods

In the end you want someone not fancy or even clean--though that would be nice--but someone good. He has to always say things he absolutely means, he has to do the things that prove the words he has spoken to you not once, but always and again, and again. To be good means he doesn't forget how to love you when you make him suffer. It means he will not let the old woman on the bus stand and wobble in the wake of every sharp turn. He will be good, he will say, Please ma'am, take my seat. If the dog is too sick to eat, to move, to even breathe, he will not hesitate, he will be good and in all that goodness, even as he buries that poor dog he will keep saying, You were a good dog, the best dog ever. When humans die he will not bring over a casserole or tell them how sorry he is for their loss, he won't use words at a time when words cruelly chew up newer ghosts. He will use his eyes and his hands; he will place a hand on a shoulder or the top of a head. He will absorb the grief; he will drive it into his bones and release it through his own tears, out into the world where the grief can breathe again, where it will find a dark kind of love.

He will touch you when you want to be touched and let you be when your hackles rise. He will be good to you, resist the urge to shackle you in guilt. He will be good in the way that he listens, because he will hear not just the things you say but the notes beneath their sounds too, and play the essence of what you speak and what you mean.

He will be too good and you will go looking for pain like you always do. You'll find pain, you'll marinate inside its stale waters, its blackened pools. You'll go so numb you will forget to even feel ashamed. You'll believe that pain is good for you. You will trouble yourself with finding new kinds of pain. You will trouble yourself.

You will remember the good you haven't found; the good that never came. The dream of that goodness rises in blue steam from the back of your neck. Your pain has been disassembled, liquefied and turned to vapors, gases that suffocate the memory of a phantom goodness.

In the end, you will want someone good. But you will choose the jagged edge of a broken rock over the smoothness of a round, naked stone. You will suffer because you believe you have to. You will choose building strength over finding peace.

41186997R00059

Made in the USA
Charleston, SC
22 April 2015